Human Habitats

LIFE BY THE OCEAN

By Holly Duhig

CRABTREE
PUBLISHING COMPANY
WWW.CRABTREEBOOKS.COM

Author:
Holly Duhig
Editorial director:
Kathy Middleton
Editors:
Emilie Dufresne
Janine Deschenes
Proofreader:
Melissa Boyce
Graphic design:
Amy Li
Katherine Berti
Print and production coordinator:
Katherine Berti

Images:
Alamy Stock Photo
Aroon Thaewchatturat: p. 11 (bottom)
Design Pics Inc: p. 18 (top)
Istockphoto
twildlife: p. 17 (top)
Getty Images
Gabriel Bouys: p. 19 (bottom)
Shutterstock
ChameleonsEye: front cover (boat)
Ijam Hairi: p. 12 (inset)
khunkorn: p. 10 (top)
kksteven: p. 14
Laboo Studio: p. 13 (bottom), 15
Nokuro: p. 23 (center right)
ronemmons: p. 9 (children)
Sky Cinema: p. 7 (house)
All other images by Shutterstock

Library and Archives Canada Cataloguing in Publication

Title: Life by the ocean / Holly Duhig.
Names: Duhig, Holly, author.
Description: Series statement: Human habitats | Includes index.
Identifiers: Canadiana (print) 20190087781 | Canadiana (ebook) 2019008779X | ISBN 9780778764786 (hardcover) | ISBN 9780778764847 (softcover) | ISBN 9781427123701 (HTML)
Subjects: LCSH: Human ecology—Juvenile literature. | LCSH: Coastal ecology—Juvenile literature. | LCSH: Marine ecology—Juvenile literature. | LCSH: Ocean and civilization—Juvenile literature. | LCSH: Dwellings—Juvenile literature.
Classification: LCC GF65 .D84 2019 | DDC j304.209162—dc23

Library of Congress Cataloging-in-Publication Data

Names: Duhig, Holly author.
Title: Life by the ocean / Holly Duhig.
Description: New York : Crabtree Publishing Company, 2019. | Series: Human habitats | Includes index. | Audience: Age 5-7. | Audience: K to Grade 3.
Identifiers: LCCN 2019014260 (print) | LCCN 2019021649 (ebook) | ISBN 9781427123701 (Electronic) | ISBN 9780778764786 (hardcover) | ISBN 9780778764847 (pbk.)
Subjects: LCSH: Ocean--Juvenile literature. | Coastal settlements--Juvenile literature. | Human ecology--Juvenile literature.
Classification: LCC GF65 (ebook) | LCC GF65 .D84 2019 (print) | DDC 304.20914/6--dc23
LC record available at https://lccn.loc.gov/2019014260

Crabtree Publishing Company
www.crabtreebooks.com 1-800-387-7650
Published by Crabtree Publishing Company in 2020

Printed in the U.S.A./072019/CG20190501

Published in Canada
Crabtree Publishing
616 Welland Ave.
St. Catharines, Ontario
L2M 5V6

Published in the United States
Crabtree Publishing
PMB 59051
350 Fifth Avenue, 59th Floor
New York, New York 10118

CRABTREE PLUS

CONTENTS

Words that look like **this** can be found in the glossary on page 24.

HUMAN HABITATS

Sharks have gills that let them get oxygen in their underwater habitat.

Animals live in habitats. They are places that provide animals with food, water, and shelter. An animal's body is adapted to its habitat.

The places humans live can also be called habitats. Humans adapt their **behavior** to survive in different habitats. For example, they can eat food that is found in the environment where they live.

Many humans live by oceans. We cannot live in them like sharks. But we can use a snorkel to breathe underwater while we swim or fish!

CAPE TOWN, SOUTH AFRICA

HABITATS BY OCEANS

The coast is the place where the land meets the ocean. People around the world live on coasts. Many depend on oceans to survive. For example, they eat food that comes from oceans.

VANCOUVER, BRITISH COLUMBIA, CANADA

SEVEN MILE BEACH, GRAND CAYMAN ISLAND

Coasts around the world are different. How people live on different coasts changes too.

KOBE, JAPAN

Superstorm Sandy destroyed many houses on the coast of the United States, such as this one in New Jersey.

Living near the ocean might sound like a lot of fun. Many people go to coasts for vacations. However, extreme weather such as floods and ocean storms can make living by the ocean difficult. To survive, people must adapt to live on coasts.

LIFE ON THE ANDAMAN SEA

There are about 800 islands in the Mergui Archipelago.

The Moken people live on islands and boats around the Mergui Archipelago. An archipelago is a group of islands. The Mergui Archipelago is in the Andaman Sea, which is part of the Indian Ocean.

The Moken people depend on the sea. They have adapted to life there. They travel by boat from island to island. Some even live on houseboats called *kabang*. They fish in the sea and gather island plants for food.

Moken people can also live in small villages on coasts.

SURVIVING BY THE SEA

As they get older, Moken people are less able to see clearly underwater.

Moken children can hold their breath underwater for a long time. They can also see clearly underwater. This makes it easier for them to dive beneath the water and find food.

The Moken people have learned to look for signs of extreme weather. In 2004, there was a huge **tsunami** in the Indian Ocean. Before the tsunami, the Moken people noticed animals acting differently and the water drawing away from the shore. They knew the tsunami would come, so they climbed to higher ground to survive.

Moken people rebuilt their villages after the tsunami.

LIFE IN THE PACIFIC OCEAN

The Sama Dilaut people live on and around the Sulu Archipelago in the Pacific Ocean, near the Philippines. Some live off the shore, in houseboats. Others live on or near coasts, in houses built on stilts.

The Sama Dilaut have adapted to life on the ocean. They eat fish from the ocean. They use the plants that grow there in different ways. For example, they use weeds from the water, rice, and spices to make *burak*. It is a powder that protects them from the Sun.

Families of Sama Dilaut people often float together on a group of boats, called a flotilla.

DIVING AND SURVIVING

This girl is searching for sea urchins. They are a good source of food.

The Sama Dilaut people are known for their diving abilities. They dive to hunt for food underwater. The Sama Dilaut can hold their breath for minutes at a time, and can dive more than 65 feet (20 m) underwater!

Diving deep underwater puts a lot of **pressure** on a person's ears. This can be painful. Some Sama Dilaut purposely damage their eardrums at a young age. This allows them to dive without pain. However, it means that they usually have difficulty hearing as adults.

LIFE ON THE ALASKAN COAST

Alaska has many miles (km) of coast by the Arctic and North Pacific Oceans. Many people live on these coasts. The ocean is a very important part of their lives.

Many people in Alaska depend on the ocean to survive.

People use boats for hunting and fishing.

The oceans by the Alaskan coast have cold waters and sea ice. Many animals live in this habitat, such as seals, sea otters, polar bears, whales, and fish. The people living on the coasts hunt these animals for food. Some people make clothing from the animals' skins and furs.

ADAPTING OVER TIME

Native Alaskan people, such as the Alutiiq, use animal skins to make warm clothing, blankets, and even crafts.

Native Alaskan groups have lived on coasts in Alaska for a very long time. In Nanwalek, Alaska, there is a village of Alutiiq people. They have adapted to life there. They built houses on high ground to avoid tsunamis. They hunt ocean animals for food and build boats to get around on the water.

The ocean water can slowly wear away the land on coasts. This is called coastal **erosion**. Coastal erosion affects communities on coasts around the world, including Alaska. As the land wears away, houses, roads, and other buildings can be destroyed. Some could fall into the water.

This home in Shishmaref, Alaska, was destroyed when the land below it wore away.

LIFE ON AN OIL RIG

Oil is used to make electricity, the energy we use to power our homes.

Oil rigs are large structures that are built far out in the ocean. From oil rigs, people **drill** deep into the **ocean floor** to reach oil.

The people who drill for oil live on the rig. Usually, they live there for a couple of weeks at a time. Around 200 people might work on an oil rig at once. They adapt to life there. For example, they sleep in small bunks and learn to stay safe when they work.

To get to and from an oil rig, people must be transported by a helicopter.

STAYING SAFE

Working on an oil rig can be dangerous. The weather can change quickly. Workers wear clothes that keep them cool in hot weather and warm in cold weather. The weather can be cold and stormy far out in the ocean.

Workers learn how to stay safe on the oil rig. They wear gear such as hard hats and safety goggles.

THINK ABOUT IT

Can you think of some other ways people adapt to live by oceans?

PEOPLE LIVING ON COASTS USE DEFENSES TO SEND WAVES BACK TO THE OCEAN.

PEOPLE WHO LIVE ON BOATS IN THE PACIFIC OCEAN LEARN TO DIVE DEEP UNDERWATER TO FIND FISH.

Many people make the ocean or the coast their human habitat. They may eat food from the ocean, live or travel on boats, or depend on it for their job. People also have found ways to adapt to extreme weather by oceans.

GLOSSARY

adapted Changed over time to suit an environment

behavior The way a person acts

drill To make a hole in something, sometimes to reach the material beneath the surface

erosion The process of something wearing away over time

Native Alaskans Indigenous peoples, or first inhabitants, of Alaska

ocean floor The bottom of the ocean

oxygen An invisible gas that all people need to survive

pressure Force put on an object by something pressing against it

stilts Long poles that hold buildings or people above the ground

Superstorm Sandy A hurricane that hit parts of the Caribbean and North America in 2012

tsunami Huge, damaging waves usually caused by earthquakes or underwater volcanic eruptions

INDEX

To learn more about human habitats around the world, enter the code at the Crabtree Plus website below.

crabtreeplus.com/humanhabitats

Your code is:
hhs12